Trinity Elementary
5th Grade

BRAVE LIKE MY BROTHER

Brave Like My Brother

Marc Tyler Nobleman

SCHOLASTIC PRESS

Library of Congress Cataloging-in-Publication Data

Nobleman, Marc Tyler, author.
Brave like my brother / Marc Tyler Nobleman.—First edition.
pages cm
Summary: When Charlie's older brother Joe is called up in
1942, Charlie learns about the tedium and dangers of war
through Joe's letters—and his brother's bravery in dealing
with a spy as D-Day approaches, finally gives Charlie the
strength to stand up to the local bully.
ISBN 978-0-545-88035-0
1. Brothers—Juvenile fiction. 2. World War,
1939–1945—Juvenile fiction. 3. Courage—Juvenile fiction.
4. Bullying—Juvenile fiction. [1. Brothers—Fiction. 2. World
War, 1939–1945—Fiction. 3. Courage—Fiction. 4. Bullying—
Fiction. 5. Letters—Fiction.] I. Title.
PZ7.N67154Br 2016
813.54—dc23
[Fic]
2015029287

10 9 8 7 6 5 4   17 18 19 20

Printed in the U.S.A.   23
First edition, July 2016

Book design by Christopher Stengel

To my brothers
by choice: Mike,
Seth, Darren,
Christian, Kevin,
Matt, and Matt

JUNE 6, 1942
CLEVELAND, OHIO

Dear Joe,

If there wasn't a war on, you'd kill me for this.

I know I'm not supposed to touch your stuff without asking. You've said it only about 10,000 times. But by the time you read this, I'll be far away. Well, you'll be far away. And anyway, you have bigger things on your mind now. So I'm not worried that you'll be sore with your kid brother for sneaking into your bag to hide this letter.

But that doesn't mean I'm not worried. I didn't want to tell you this before you left, but I AM worried. A lot. Who wouldn't be? Dad and Uncle Fred's World War I stories are pretty scary. I just don't want you to go to England. I wish the Japanese hadn't bombed Pearl Harbor. Then maybe America wouldn't have gotten caught up in this cockeyed war and you wouldn't have to go anywhere farther than work (and the movies, when Mom forces you to take me).

I know I get on your nerves, so I bet you won't miss me as much as I'll miss you. But something tells me that you WILL miss me.

You give me a hard time sometimes just because that's what big brothers have to do. But if you didn't like having me for a brother, you wouldn't have stuck up for me those times when Jed was making fun of me because I'd rather read than run around causing trouble like he does. I probably didn't thank you for that before you left, or ever; so thanks, Joe. I couldn't believe when you told me that Jed was one of the only guys from your class who wasn't drafted. Why didn't they take him instead of you?

Even though you think you'll be no good as a soldier, I'm already proud of you. Now is my chance to try to make you proud of me. I'm going to do my best to do what you asked me to do when you're gone. And I hope you will do something for me, too.

Come back the same.

Love,

Charlie

June 9, 1942
Halfway across the
Atlantic Ocean

Dear Charlie,

You beat me to it. I found your letter as I was getting settled on the boat. It's weird to be writing you a letter. Okay, for me, it's weird to be writing ANYONE a letter. But especially you, since we've lived under the same roof since the day you were born.

Here I come, England. (Or United Kingdom. Not sure the difference but guess I'm about to find out.)

Sure, you're a pest sometimes, but of course I'm going to miss you. And Mom and Dad. Even my job at Milton's. But that luncheonette is going to miss me more, since I'm the first halfway decent cook they've hired in a while. Only two weeks after I start working there, I'm called to duty. Rotten timing.

This all happened so fast. I hear guys who enlisted got parties thrown for them before they left home. Lucky stiffs. All we get is a phone call: "Report in three days." That's too long to wait for the unknown and too short to say a proper good-bye.

Imperial Japan to our left, Nazi Germany to our right. No fun to be surrounded. Who knows where I'll end up? I don't know if

I'll be able to mail a letter every day, but I'm going to write you every day. At least I'm sure going to try. Hope you can write me, too. You're a lot better with words than me, so I'm getting the better deal. Sorry about that, pal.

Charlie, please don't worry about me. It may not show all the time, but I've probably gained SOME wisdom in my life so far. You just worry about being a kid—let the grown-ups handle this mess of a war. While I won't be around to look out for you, just avoid Jed and those other chumps who get their kicks picking on smaller kids. I told them to leave you alone, but guys with small brains have short memories. Maybe that's why Jed wasn't drafted. But then, why was I?

Most important, look out for Mom and Dad. Course Mom's busy taking care of Grandma, and Dad's busy working like always, but they'll need you more than they'll let on. Stay positive and Mom and Dad may follow your lead. Not what ten-year-olds normally have to do, but these aren't normal times. If life were fair, I'd be making hot roast beef sandwiches for the lunch rush right now.

Love,
Private Joe Fuller
AKA your big brother

Dear Charlie,

First day of summer, first day of England, first day of war.

The boat we took here sure looked big from the pier, but once we were inside, it made a sardine tin look roomy. It was so crowded that half the time, we had to eat standing up. Breakfast was often boiled eggs that were, for some reason, gray. But worst was the kippered herrings. If you don't know

9

what that is, trust me, don't ask. Compared to military fare so far, Milton's grub is fit for the Queen of England.

Guys were throwing up left and right, sometimes from the choppiness and sometimes, I bet, because the food is so bad. Being near a guy who's heaving is never fun, but especially when you're packed in so tight that you can't escape the smell. It was a rough ride, but it's nothing compared to what is in store for us now.

In our letters, we're not allowed to be too specific about a lot of things, including where exactly we are or where we're going. I can say that our port of entry was Liverpool, which I'd never heard of. Me not hearing of a place is no shock. You got the brains in the family.

But did you know that the United Kingdom is smaller than California?

For a guy who had never been past Cleveland city limits, this is almost too much to take in. It's like half fairy tale, half war machine—pretty and grim at once.

But I'm not the only rube here. All of us were issued a little book called *Instructions for American Servicemen in Britain 1942*. I never stopped to realize how little I know about British people. And I really didn't think about how they must feel about us coming here now. After all, they've been holding off Hitler and the Nazis all by themselves for two years. They're not exactly damsels in distress.

We got a nice welcome—you should have

seen the tasty dishes waving to us as we disembarked. (Maybe men were there, too—only you don't notice when so many pretty girls are making eyes at you.) But as the instruction guide says, "Remember that crossing the ocean doesn't automatically make you a hero."

Hope you, Mom, and Dad are holding up alright.

Love,

Joe

June 29, 1942
Great Britain

Dear Charlie,

So glad to get your letter, pal. So far, sunshine is as rare here as a barking cat, but news from home can warm us up even better.

I just hope you're telling the truth, that things are as fine as can be under the circumstances. But if you're saying that just so I don't worry, please tell it to me straight. I can take it. Or let's put it this way—I have to take it. It's easier than wondering.

So I'm not two-faced, I have to tell you that things here are, well, tough and getting tougher. We've moved south for training and it's a bleak place—nothing but nothing as far as the eye can see. Boondocksville. Some of the guys get to stay in Nissen huts, these small, simple quarters made of steel with a curved roof, but most of us are stuck in tents. And stuck TO us all is an enemy no one saw coming.

We train on large fields of dirt, but since it rains a lot, it all turns to thick, sloppy mud. It clogs our shoes, clings to our clothes, sticks in our pores, and even gets in our mouths, though the food we're served doesn't always taste much better. (They do give us more

candy than we can eat, and no one is com-
plaining about that.)

And there's something else here that's really
aggravating. His name is Matthew Sower,
pride and joy of Elkhorn, Nebraska. This guy
finds something to criticize about everyone,
except our superior officers. He and Jed would
be fast friends. He looks down on the city
folk because they "don't know how to survive
in the real world." He says nasty things about
the colored guys even though they're here
defending a country that doesn't cut them a
break. Me, he makes a joke out of the fact
that I like to cook. He said, "You should've
stayed home with the ladies." I want to knock
the guy around, but that's not really me.

Matt thinks growing up in the heartland with its harsh winters and barren stretches of land makes him cut out to be a soldier more than the rest of us. He acts like he's the only one with any life experience before this. Cleveland isn't exactly a stroll down the beach. The sooner he and I are put on different squads won't be soon enough.

We're starting to hear stories about the Nazis that are worse than what they report in the States. I don't want to bring you down. Just don't believe everything you read.

War is just life with bigger bullies.

I miss you, pal.

Love,

Joe

Dear Charlie,

Thanks for your latest letter. And thanks for being honest with me. I'm steamed to hear that those fatheads in the neighborhood haven't respected my wishes. It burns me up that they tease you. I wish I could do something from here. I've got the army to make more of a man out of me, but you'll have to do that yourself for the time being. I know it isn't easy, even talking about it isn't easy, but

I have faith in you. You may not be bigger than Jed and his cronies, but you're sure smarter.

Think of Superman. You mention his adventures in almost every letter, so you're probably already thinking about him. Or better, think of his creators. I had no idea those guys live in Cleveland. You said they've been pushed around, too, been made fun of and rejected, but despite that, look what they accomplished.

Training has us up before sunrise and beats us up by breakfast. They're teaching us hand-to-hand combat with real knives. No one's been jabbed yet, but it's only a matter of time.

Plus it rains—often pours—almost daily. We're wet pretty much all of the time. And just when we thought we couldn't get any wetter, we had to practice river crossings.

For a week straight, they made us run everywhere—meals, bathroom, showers. You can imagine how the mud made this even more fun. We've been sent on long hikes—again, in the rain—and had to find our way back in the dark.

One time, when we were already over-due, Matt swore he knew the way back, that he was used to this kind of thing. How, I don't know, since back home he works at a furniture store. This nice guy from New Hampshire, Ira, has worked at a camp for five summers, so he knows a thing or two about the outdoors, but he didn't need to show off about it. Matt told us, "You'd be stupid not to trust me." So we did. And he only ended up taking us in circles.

Then when we finally did reach the camp, he blamed US—said he was trying to show us how to think for ourselves, and we failed. I think he was just trying to cover up that HE was the stupid one in this case. Well, maybe not stupid, but not wise enough to own up to a mistake. Later, Ira told me he hadn't said anything when Matt wanted to take charge, so that our commanding officers would see that Matt should NOT take charge.

Some of the equipment we have to use dates back to World War I. Guess they can't afford to buy new models. Happy to help Uncle Sam save a buck or two, but if any of this gear has gone to seed over the past twenty-five years, it's going to cost some of our boys more than that.

We had our first weekend furlough. That's a break, and we sure needed one. Me, Ira, and a fella with a super sense of humor named Francisco followed the stampede of other Americans from all over Great Britain and headed to London. What a town!

Getting there looking presentable posed a small problem. Being that our camp is in a moor, you can't walk anywhere around it without your boots getting caked with mud. So we put wool socks over our clean shoes, trudged to the nearest paved road, stripped off the dirty socks, left them there, and caught a ride to the train to get us to the city. Everyone does it. I said the side of that road is a sock graveyard. Francisco said, "That's what I call the inside of Matt's head." Like I told you, Francisco's a funny guy.

Turns out American soldiers are earning at least four times as much money as British soldiers. Turns out the Brits don't much like this. In the pubs (what we call taverns or bars), the Brits make us feel guilty and they seem jealous of us when we talk to British girls. But we're not forcing anyone to do anything. I am pretty sure the girls like our accents as much as we like theirs! They say we remind them of Hollywood movies. I don't know a soldier who doesn't like to hear that.

One night in a pub, Matt tapped the shoulder of a British soldier at the next table and said, "America can win the war without your help." Our guide urges us to respect local culture, and Matt had to go and act like the rules don't apply to him. The Brit said that England didn't ask for help, even when the Germans were bombing London night after night, and he, for one, was not asking for help now.

Matt looked around and said, "I don't see any British commanders asking us to leave the country." The other British soldiers at the table put down their pints and stood. They were ready for a fight.

Matt stood, too. When I reminded them that we're on the same team, Matt laughed.

But when he realized none of us were going to stand by him, he stormed out. All I heard him say was, "The Brits have enough problems."

I apologized to the soldier but it didn't matter, since it didn't come from Matt. So much for us Americans being gracious guests.

But London wasn't all awkward situations. British children are also quite fond of American soldiers. They followed us around and surrounded us when we stopped, asking, "Got any gum, chum?" (The girls like us for our accents, the kids for our candy.) They've been living under strict rations—meaning the government limits how much you can buy— so even a small gift is a big deal to them. We also played a few street games with the kids.

Some of the boys reminded me of you. Actually, just about all of them did.

Love to Mom and Dad. Hope Grandma is managing, and hope you are, too.

Love,

Joe

August 13, 1942
Mud Britain

Dear Censor,

I hope you're leaving my letters intact. I know you're supposed to look for info that could put the troops in danger and also for signs of a hole in morale, but aside from my issues with Matt Sower, and aside from my grumblings about mud and exhaustion, I'm honored to be serving my country and don't want to put our efforts at risk. As for Matt,

I'm sure there are guys here that YOU think are a pain in the neck.

Dear Charlie,

Sorry about that. Just had to talk to the Man with the Black Pen for a second.

Hey, are you getting letters from me with parts crossed out? Did you get my letters of July 30 and July 18? Maybe they're not just crossing out lines that cause concern. Maybe they're discarding the whole letter.

Speaking of morale, thanks for doing what you can to boost Mom and Dad's. Trust me, you're the biggest source of comfort for them. The more you can tell them that I mean it when I say I'm okay, the more chocolate bars

I'll take home for you. Yes, that's a bribe, but a fair one, I think.

Good on you for sticking up for yourself! Most bullies are cowards in disguise. So the kid just turned tail and walked away, no more knuckleheaded remarks? Any sign of Jed?

Most bullies are cowards in disguise, but who knows what disguise—if any—cowards hide behind. I may find out before long. (Mr. Censor, I'm not talking about myself.)

Love,
Joe

P.S. No other update of note. Just more manuevers, moors, mud, Matt, and missing home. Have you eaten at Milton's lately? How's my replacement working out? Probably not living up to my shoes, or whatever the expression is. Want to go in and ask him if he wants to switch places with me? Ha-ha.

September 13, 1942
Rainy Old England

Dear Charlie,

Thanks for more home front news. Sorry Mom's cooking hasn't improved since I left. If she'll let me, I'll give her some more lessons when I get back.

You're a strong kid, pal, to stand up to those crumbs who don't know when to lay off. They're just threatened by you because you're good in school. Maybe their fathers or brothers are over here, and it's upsetting them, and the way they try to stop being afraid is by acting tough in front of others. I'm not excusing them, but I can understand.

It was really nice of you to say I'm a role model for you, Charlie, but I don't know how that can be. I only stood up for a little kid in broad daylight against a guy who's no bigger than me. That doesn't take courage. No offense. Besides, even though I told those guys to let you be, they didn't. I tell Matt to quit trying to get a rise out of me and he doesn't. A war-within-a-war almost breaks out in a pub and all I do is flap my lips. I'm better working with food. Food doesn't fight.

We've been wet all summer and now we're cold, too. The moors bring down a fierce wind at times. To prevent soggy bottoms, sometimes we try to sleep sitting up on our helmets. That was Ira's idea. He's got lots of tricks like that. Francisco said we can't let the enemy know this or else they might call us "butts-for-brains." If only all our problems were that minor. Even though we can laugh about it, some nights it feels like we will never be comfortable again.

After the pub incident, Matt glares at me more than before, as if it was my fault, or as if he thought I should have sided with him. Now I talk to him as little as possible.

But funny as it sounds, competing with Matt during training is making us both better soldiers. We try to outdo the other. Captain Bunt doesn't tolerate the boys arguing among ourselves—it distracts everyone.

So he must be keeping Matt and me close to each other for a reason.

Outside of letters from Ohio, the biggest light of the day is Cookie. A few days ago, out here in the middle of nowhere, this ragged but friendly dog showed up. We all took to him right away, and he took to us—particularly to Matt. Who knows, maybe they're long-lost brothers. No, I don't want to insult Cookie.

That name was suggested by Matt, by the way, and no one objected. I actually like it, but I didn't tell him that.

Love,

Joe

Dear Charlie,

My first holiday season away. Thanksgiving is always the one time of year everyone focuses on each other. Dad's not working, Mom's busy at home. This year I hope you were twice as chatty at the table, to get their minds off the fact that I'm not there.

I was with a mom and a dad, just not ours (obviously). Many Brits invited Yanks to dinner for Thanksgiving. In fact, most of us got more than one invitation. Our superior officers encouraged us to share some of our own rations and care packages with our hosts. (We'd do that anyway.) The locals are really suffering under the rationing here. I brought my hosts a can of peas and they reacted like it was prime rib. Their regular diet is Brussels sprouts, Spam, and mutton, so any break from that is worth getting excited about.

We were also told not to eat too much, even if our host family set out a big, swell spread of food. Mine did—even opened and served my peas right then. They didn't let on about it, but our dinner might have been their entire rations for a week. More than kind under conditions like theirs.

No turkey, though. We're all making the best of it, Americans and Brits alike.

Ira's family said he looked like Jimmy Stewart from *Mr. Smith Goes to Washington.* I guess he thought that was a compliment. Francisco told his family the "butts-for-brains" story just to hear them repeat "butts-for-brains" in a British accent. And in the spirit of the season, I can say that Matt's not all bad. He got a letter from HIS brother and I saw a tear in his eye. He saw me see him, and I just nodded. Rather than puff up his chest, he nodded back. Progress, I guess.

Being in a war zone shows a guy that the list of things he's thankful for is a lot longer than he realized.

I'm thankful that we're not yet in combat. We wake up each morning not knowing if that's the day we will be thrown into battle. It wears down a fella's nerves.

I'm thankful (and not surprised) that Grandma is showing just how tough she is, even though I know she's in pain. She lived through the first war with no fear, didn't she?

Most of all, I'm thankful you send as many letters as you do. You're the cable connecting me to my real life.

I'll spare you the rest of my list.

Love,

Joe

March 2, 1943
3,500 miles east

Dear Charlie,

Soon that will be 3,700 miles. I'm being sent on a mission.

With Matt.

Captain Bunt has observed how Matt and I lock horns. So he assigned the two of us—only the two of us—to attempt this mission together. Jimmy Stewart and Butts-for-Brains asked me to send them a postcard from our "vacation." Why couldn't one of them come with me instead?

Matt and I asked Bunt if we could take Cookie. Bunt said no—he said a dog is too much of a wild card and could put us in jeopardy. He's right. But I still would like to take him.

Got to keep this one short—we leave tonight.

I can't say where we're going. I don't KNOW where we're going.

I know you think you're learning about the war from comic books as much as my letters, but whatever story they're telling, the reality's worse.

I sure wouldn't mind seeing your pal Superman in the flesh right about now.

Love,

Joe

Dear Charlie,

Oh boy, has a lot happened since last I wrote.

A few weeks ago, Matt and I set out after dark on the mission. We'd been around each other all the time, but it wasn't till then when I realized we'd never been ALONE together. I tried to start over with him, find common ground, like the fact that we're both big brothers. But he preferred to bust the chops of other guys in our company, even though they weren't there to defend themselves. They wouldn't care, but still, I didn't want to hear him point out faults in my friends. I asked him about his brother, but all I got was that his name is Richard and he's fifteen years old.

Our ride was a military Jeep and our cargo was in the back, covered by a tarp that was secured with hooks. We were told not to look under the tarp. We were supposed to transport the cargo to a camp in southeastern England. Under normal circumstances, that would be a five-hour drive . . . you can already guess where this is headed.

I took the first shift driving. Aside from our headlights, the world around us was black as watermelon seeds. Not long after we left, I heard an unusual noise in back, like breathing. I asked Matt if he'd heard it, too, and he said he did and would check it out. As I kept driving, he turned around and leaned into the backseat. "All clear," he said. Maybe a dog running loose, he said.

A short while later, I heard it again. I stopped the car and checked the back myself. Matt just sat there holding back a smile. But when I found the source of the sound, I couldn't help but smile myself. It WAS a dog—it was Cookie. Matt had smuggled the dog into the transport. I have to admit I was impressed he sneaked this past Captain Bunt. But I was also annoyed. Though it was

Matt who had disobeyed an order, if Bunt found out, I'd get in trouble, too. Matt just told me to relax.

We gave Cookie some affection, then got back on the road—if you can call muddy countryside crisscrossed with barbed-wire fences a "road." Just when I thought Matt had nodded off, he said, "My dog died." Then he proceeded to tell me more about his beagle, Tumbler, than he'd ever said about all the human beings in his family combined. I joked before that Matt might be half dog, but now I half believe it. Matt and I still quarreled, but having Cookie with us did ease some of the stress.

Matt asked what I thought we had under

the tarp. I said I didn't have a guess and didn't care. I asked what he thought it was. He said a bomb.

Joe

April 7, 1943

Dear Charlie,

Busy days here. Sorry I had to cut my last letter short—so short I couldn't even TELL you I was cutting it short. So, here is what happened next.

England goes into blackout mode at night, meaning that they make everyone turn off the lights in their homes so they're not easy targets for enemy planes. During our drive, we passed a few towns, but since they were blacked out, sometimes we barely noticed them. When we saw what looked like a long, straight, clear stretch ahead, we turned our headlights off, too. Driving blind is nuts, but it beats getting blown to bits.

Not long after I discovered Cookie the stowaway, I began to feel funny. We couldn't have been an hour and a half into the drive. I thought maybe the constant cold and damp had finally made me sick. Matt took over the driving. Course he had to say, "Don't think you can get out of your next shift just because you say you're not feeling well." As if I were lying.

When I began to tremble, I wondered aloud if we should contact our company—or any company. Our Jeep was outfitted with a humdinger of a machine—a two-way radio that could allow us to talk to a base up to fifteen miles away. As much as I wanted to try it at first, Matt and I agreed that it wasn't a good idea—what if someone on the wrong side intercepted the message? I just tried to think away how I was feeling. Didn't work.

And that wasn't even the worst of the night.

At one point, with our headlights off, Matt hit a ditch. We both banged our heads against the roof of the Jeep, but we weren't going fast enough that it hurt. Still, it did pop a tire. Changing a flat in the dark is not easy. Changing a flat when you're feeling lousy is no fun. And changing a flat with Matt might be more awful than both of them. No matter what is going on, he has to be the one who knows better. I just let him. I didn't need to prove anything.

While Matt worked on the tire, Cookie began barking. At first it made no sense, but then we saw why—a flashlight. It STILL made no sense . . . who would be walking out there at that time of night, during wartime? But someone was definitely approaching.

We both pulled our handguns. A voice called out that he was lost. British accent. I shined my flashlight on him. He was in civilian clothes and looked scared. He stopped right near the rear of our vehicle, near the cargo. I asked him how he found himself here and he said his car ran out of fuel, so he was trying to find a petrol station.

But petrol was rationed—for official use only, like the military. Something wasn't right.

So I asked if he was a soldier and he said, "We're all playing our part, aren't we?"

I could tell Matt was suspicious, too, but far as we could figure, this man wasn't doing anything wrong at the moment. We said we didn't know where the nearest village was. He thanked us and turned to leave. We turned back to the tire—Matt fixing, me watching. I asked Matt if he thought it was strange that the man didn't ask us for a ride, and just then there was a flash behind us.

He took a photograph!

Then we heard running into the distance.

Matt said "Spy!" and bolted up to give chase. I grabbed his arm and said that if it

WAS a photo, it couldn't have captured any-thing important—the tarp was fully covering whatever we were transporting. Matt jerked his arm away and tore off after the guy. I was so wobbly I couldn't go after HIM. A few minutes later, Matt returned. He was furi-ous at me for trying to stop him, and furious at himself for failing to stop the photogra-pher. I said our priority is the mission—and we were already delayed.

But then we heard planes overhead. We quickly killed the lights in the Jeep and waited it out. Matt dozed off and I reread some of your letters by flashlight.

More later.

How are you, buddy? Still taking good care of Mom and Dad, I trust? I know that's hard, but it's for your own good, too. I'm so sorry I left, Charlie. I want to promise that I won't do it again, but I'm afraid to, in case I can't live up to that promise.

Love,

Joe

April 26, 1943
Top Secret Location, UK

Dear Charlie,

Thanks for writing me such great letters, pal. They lift me up. And for once, I might have a story that will lift you up. Your brother had a brush with greatness.

After the spy got away and Matt conked out in the Jeep, I was going back over some of the letters you've sent me. Think I told you that. I felt so weak. Next thing I know, there's a rap at the window—and it's morning. An

American infantry platoon, maybe forty guys, had come upon us and clearly thought we were a couple of dopes for sleeping on the job. At one point I would have said they were only half right (meaning Matt), but I was guilty as charged, too. By sleeping through the night, we lost HOURS. And I didn't wake up feeling any better.

Their lieutenant chewed us out, and he had every right to. I handed him our orders, part of which were sealed in an envelope we were not to open ourselves. After reading them, he notified our superior officer as to where we were and decided not to write up a report on us. He did strongly order us to get a move on.

But before we could, another military

caravan came into view—and there was something different about it. That turned out to be an understatement.

One of the men in the caravan was Eisenhower himself.

GENERAL DWIGHT D. EISENHOWER. I knew he had made it a point to personally meet every Allied division—every group of American soldiers—but I had no idea he wasn't still fighting in North Africa. Maybe this was just a short, secret side mission. Either way, all of us were made to stand in a row while Eisenhower walked along it, passing every man. I'm glad the lieutenant didn't tell General Eisenhower that Matt and I were not in that platoon and that we had just gotten in trouble. Eisenhower said something to each soldier.

To me he said, "I salute your service to your country, son." Maybe that was what he said to everyone. In any case, then and there, I got a new sense of commitment to the war.

As the general was stepping back into his vehicle, Cookie took it upon himself to start barking. I thought we'd be chewed out again for sure. But you'll never guess what happened. Eisenhower got out of the car and went up to our Jeep. He opened the door . . . and petted Cookie on the head!

Then he said "As you were, soldier." (Yes, he said that to a DOG.) I didn't dare turn to look to Matt but if I had, I bet it would have been one of the rare moments when we smiled at each other.

Eisenhower left, and Matt and I left, too. We had hours to go in our journey to deliver the mystery cargo.

Love,

Joe

June 15, 1943

Dear Charlie,

Sorry for the delay in writing.

You joked that you did not believe my Eisenhower story (that WAS a joke, right?), but here's one you are NOT going to believe even more than that.

While entering a small town for the first time on the trip, I still felt feverish, and then also sick to my stomach. So much so that I asked Matt to stop the car so I could get out, lean over, and throw up. Which I did, and quite nicely, I must say. Matt did not miss the chance to put me down for not being able to "handle war."

When I stood up, two things happened at once. First, I felt better. Second, I saw someone walking nearby who looked familiar. It took me a moment to realize it was the man who'd come up to us when we had the flat tire—the mystery photographer. What happened last time was bizarre. This time, it was plain bonkers.

Mr. Bad News saw me, too, and ran toward the town square. I sprinted after him. I was surprised by my own energy. I don't know if it was because I had just puked up whatever had been slowing me down or because that time, I DID want to prove something to Matt—who had jumped from the car to follow me following the spy.

I caught up to him and grabbed him by the back of his coat. He was my size and I managed to hold on to him, asking him who he was. He was angry now, swearing that he was nobody and insisting that I let him go. I told him, "Nobodies don't run away." Then Matt arrived and shoved Mr. Bad News out of my grip and against a wall. A crowd was gathering now.

Matt asked why he had taken a photo of us. The man said nothing. Matt shouted at him, demanding the truth. The man denied knowing what we were talking about and looked around, maybe for someone to help him.

Matt balled a fist to wallop the guy, and I did it again—I tried to stop him. But Matt wasn't having it that time—he turned around and hit ME in the head. I had my helmet on, so it didn't hurt too much.

In the chaos, Mr. Bad News pulled out a gun. In a split second, Matt was on him again, trying to wrestle the gun from his hand. MBN dropped the gun but slammed Matt into a stone pillar of a building. Matt cried out and grabbed his arm. In the confusion, MBN picked up his gun and aimed it at Matt's head.

I pounced on MBN, knocking us both to the ground. He still had the gun, though. A shot went off, but over my head. The crowd scattered, shrieking. I elbowed MBN in the chest and knocked the wind out of him. Then I twisted his hand till he let go of the gun.

I raised my hand over his face and he called out—in German. Up till then, he'd spoken British English with no trace of an accent. At least he got THAT part of spy training right.

I didn't think I had it in me. I'm not bragging. This wasn't much. But it was more than I thought I could do.

Though Matt was in pain, he helped me subdue the spy. We tied his hands behind his back. But then we had no idea what to do next. We'd been trained to deal with soldiers, not spies. And we were, again, sidetracked from what we were supposed to be doing.

We decided to bring him to the local police, but they turned us away. Seems they were even less able to deal with this than we were. Or they just didn't want to get mixed up in US Army business.

So we were stuck with the spy.

Meanwhile, Matt's wrist was swelling. I was guessing it was broken. That meant I would be driving the rest of the way.

We got the spy into the Jeep. He didn't have the camera on him and we didn't find out what he did with the photo he took. He would not answer any questions, just mumbled to himself in German.

Matt said, "If you're not going to tell us your name, then we're going to give you a name: Cuckoo." I guess he thought it was funny that we now had a Cookie and a Cuckoo. In my mind, I continued to call him Mr. Bad News.

But something funny DID happen—it was a bonding moment, too. Before we set out, Matt and I prepared Mr. Bad News in case he escaped. We have this pen with ink that is really hard to wash off. We used it to write "spy" many times on his face and arms. I can only chuckle when I think what Francisco would have added. And, for good measure, we also shaved the word into the hair on the back of his head.

That's something the army does NOT teach you.

We tried to stabilize Matt's injury. But as I drove, his pain got worse, to the point that he passed out. But first, he said a word I don't remember hearing from him before: "Thanks." He never apologized for decking me, though.

Love,

Joe

July 19, 1943

Dear Charlie,

I feel like all I do in these letters is talk about myself. How are YOU? Have you spotted the Superman guys around town yet? Jerry and Joe? (Nice name!) I'm stunned that they drafted Jerry. If Superman's writer is not safe, no one is.

Any new neighborhood adventures to report? Has Mom stopped crying at night? It rips me up to think of her like that. You're smart as ever, Charlie. I know I never have to tell you what not to tell Mom and Dad. The letters I write them are the less scary version of my stories. They worry enough as it is.

I guess I have no choice but to talk about myself again now. I DO keep getting interrupted. Are my letters as exciting as movie serials—one cliffhanger after another?

As I drove Matt, the dog, and the spy to our destination, the spy tried to look into the back. But we'd tied his hands to the door handle in such a way that he could barely turn his head—besides, the tarp was still pinned down tight, so he wouldn't be able to tell whatever it was anyway.

He caught me looking at him in the mirror

and spit on the back of my head. You just have to take it.

A song came on the radio. Maybe you've heard it—it's called "You'd Be So Nice to Come Home To." It's a man talking about his wife or girlfriend, but it made me think of you. Don't worry—the lyrics don't sound too sappy. I would love nothing more than to be there and cook a big breakfast for you and the family.

Aside from Mr. Bad News trying to peek at our cargo, all was easygoing. But it wasn't long before we got into our next pickle.

A storm blew in, and it was stronger than any storm I'd seen since I've been here. The rain was shooting down every which way.

The sky ate the sun and the wind sounded like spooked horses. The ground was already damp and this turned it into a scene you would not believe. We were close but hours behind schedule and now this . . . the Jeep got stuck.

We would have to get out and push. Matt's wrist made him useless, plus now he'd developed a fever, so I was on my own . . . unless I made Mr. Bad News push as well. But to do that, he'd need his hands, which meant he'd be free to do more than push if he wanted to. Even in that storm, he might be crazy enough to try to run off—he had acted crazy before. It wasn't worth taking that chance. So I pushed alone. And, of course, that didn't work.

The storm showed no sign of letting up. That left us with no option. We had to go the rest of the way on foot, even though it would be slow going. No other vehicle could get to us any quicker, so we didn't even bother radioing for help.

Once out of the car, Matt began shivering pretty bad. Maybe his injury had lowered his defenses. Maybe he'd caught what I'd had. Either way, he needed more warmth and we had nothing.

Nothing except the tarp.

I could either get in more trouble for disobeying the order to leave the tarp alone, or I could let Matt freeze to death.

At first it was a tough choice. But as

irritating as Matt had been, I wasn't about to watch him die.

So with rain pouring and Matt shaking and the spy still tied to the car door, I took off the tarp. Let's see what the censor does with this letter before I tell you the rest.

(Told you I'm good for a cliffhanger.)

Love,

Joe

July 28, 1943

Dear Charlie,

I haven't gotten a letter from you since my last, so with no questions from you to answer, I'll pick up where I left off.

Under the tarp was not a bomb and not anything else I could have expected. It was a bundle of what looked like rubber, packed tight. It took me more than a few seconds to figure out what it was, because it was something I'd never seen or even heard of before: an inflatable tank.

Holy mackerel, an inflatable tank! One that inflates to the size of a REAL tank.

I had nothing else to use as a substitute for the tarp. Leaving the fake tank exposed was a risk.

I didn't want Mr. Bad News to suspect it was anything unusual, so I tried to act like I hadn't just been completely surprised. I got Matt out and draped the tarp over his head and shoulders. I tied it across his chest, since he couldn't use his hurt hand to hold it. It wasn't particularly comfortable but it would keep him mostly dry.

In a whisper, he asked me what was under the tarp. I told him and he didn't know what to make of it, either.

I thought the best way I could try to prevent

the spy from making a break for it was to tie him to the heaviest thing coming with us— me. I was again worried that he could cause some damage if I wasn't careful.

So I tied him to me in a nutty series of steps. Before untying his hands from the Jeep door, I tied his feet together so he couldn't run. I tied a longer rope from EACH of his hands to the door, then untied the original rope connecting his hands to each other and to the door. Pulling on the two longer ropes like he was a marionette, I forced him onto the ground, facedown.

Kneeling with my full weight on his back and neck, I tugged both of his hands behind his back so I could retie them to each other there. I looped that rope around his neck so if he struggled, he'd choke himself. I untied the other ends of the longer ropes from the door.

I helped him stand and attached a rope from his bound hands to my waist. I wasn't about to untie the rope binding his feet together, but I did loosen it a little. Making him walk like this would slow us down even more, but it was the only way to prevent him from getting away. He cursed at me the whole time. At least I think it was cursing.

It was a lot of pressure . . . taking care of Matt, taking care that Mr. Bad News didn't get away, and getting both of them (plus me and Cookie) to the camp with no more pitfalls. Not to mention abandoning our cargo.

I tell you, Charlie, I didn't think I could do it.

Even with all I did with the ropes, MBN still tried to break free. At one point, my boot got stuck in the muck and right away he tried to trip me. MBN fell down on purpose to drag me down. Maybe he knew I had a knife in a side pocket of my pants and he thought he could get it.

Cookie was barking but MBN wasn't afraid of him. My rope didn't do anything to stop MBN but he couldn't get at me with his hands.

We struggled on the ground—I think he was trying to use his whole body to push my face in the mud—but it was too slippery. Matt tried to pull him off me but he had so little strength.

I was finally able to get him under control by using the binding that tied him to me. I pulled it, twisting his arms tighter behind his back. He was kicking at air and shouting. That's when Matt found some reserve of power and kicked MBN across the face.

Matt shouted, "Enough! We're late and my hand is killing me!"

Whether or not the spy understood the words, he sure understood the rage. I don't have that kind of rage. But I'm glad Matt did.

We trudged on. All of us except Cookie were in some kind of discomfort. It took close to two unpleasant hours, but filthy, battered, and bone-tired, we finally made it.

Love,

Joe

Dear Charlie,

(continued from last letter)

When we got to the camp, the captain did not thank me for helping Matt. He did not thank Matt and me for capturing a spy. No, he mainly focused on the cargo we left behind. He was NOT happy. I do understand that, but to me, a hunk of rubber is not as important as human lives.

"No single soldier is worth compromising a mission," the captain said.

That's the army for you. But the mission wasn't ruined—the cargo had not even fallen into enemy hands. At least, we didn't think it had.

The spy DID help us, though. Because we were able to get him to camp, our punishments were not as harsh as they would normally be for messing up a mission—mostly some additional duties, which Matt couldn't do right away anyway. His wrist WAS broken and a medic fixed him up. He wouldn't be sent into combat till it healed.

The captain needed two soldiers to drive out to the Jeep and retrieve the cargo, but it had to wait till the next day when the weather had cleared or else they, too, would have gotten stuck. I asked if I could do it, since I made the mistake in the first place. The captain agreed. To my surprise, Matt volunteered to go with me. He would be of no use physically, but could keep watch while I slid the cargo from one trunk to another.

What had seemed like such a long, tough journey in the rain and mud took only a few minutes in sunshine. Like the storm, Matt's tolerance for me had also passed. He made a couple of rude remarks, such as how we wouldn't be in this jam if it weren't for my decision to walk.

You're welcome for saving your life, Matt, or at least your wrist. Besides, it wasn't like HE had said it was a bad idea.

The cargo was still there. I don't know why I thought anyone would come across it, considering where we left it. Still, it being untouched meant no extra punishment for us.

Once we got back to camp, we found out what that inflatable tank (which weighs only ninety-three pounds!) is for. It is a wild story. But I can't tell you yet.

One thing I CAN tell you: We're preparing for something big.

Love,

Joe

October 10, 1943

Dear Charlie,

I'm so sad about Grandma. But I'm glad she didn't suffer in the end. I wrote Mom a long letter. She already feels like she's lost a son, and now she's lost her mother, too. But she was spending so much time helping Grandma that she never had time for herself. So maybe this will be some kind of relief for her. Is that a horrible thing to say?

So much about my life in Ohio seems like only a dream now. Milton's, the neighborhood, even the sound of your voice—the memories aren't so clear anymore. It's been only a year and a few months, but war makes each day last a week.

Matt's wrist is mostly healed. The closer we get to our larger mission—which the commanders are still keeping us boys mostly in the dark about—the more I see a side of Matt he didn't really show before. He's scared. I can tell because he's finally talking about his life back home.

Out of nowhere, he told me a story about his brother, Richard, about how he once got his arm stuck between fence posts. It was just the two of them there. At first, Matt just laughed at him, but then Richard stopped crying. Yes, STOPPED. He was still scared—but he wanted to show his big brother that he wasn't. And that was when Matt helped get Richard's arm out.

I don't know why Matt shared that story with me. Or maybe I do. But he wouldn't confirm or deny it if I asked, so I didn't bother.

I don't blame Matt for being scared. We all are. Even Cookie. He ran off and hasn't come back.

Soon we'll wish all we had to deal with was mud, bad food, and lone spies.

On top of pushing us harder on our daily training exercises, now they're teaching us a foreign language. Can't tell you which one, because it's where we're going next. Word is, the censors are so overworked that they're missing stuff in letters, so maybe I COULD tell you and they wouldn't notice. Or maybe they'd miss it just because my handwriting is famously bad—remember when Grandma said you're the only one who can read it?

Sometimes I feel like you're the only one who can read ME. Thanks for listening, always.

Love,

Joe

December 7, 1943

Dear Charlie,

Pearl Harbor was two years ago today. Some of the boys are mumbling that if not for that, we would be home with our families for the holidays. They're right, but what's the point? It happened, we're here, there's no way back, and there's only one way forward.

This anniversary and the thought of what's

next has had some kind of effect on Matt. First thing this morning, before we were ordered to crawl into small holes and sit there for hours, the way we might have to do on a battlefield, Matt told me something. It turns out that he had suggested naming the dog Cookie as a way to tease me about being a cook. I hadn't realized. Even if I had, it wouldn't have been any more obnoxious than anything else he's said or done. But then he said the joke was too dumb to be mean. He got that right!

And then—get this—he asked about YOU. He asked how you're doing with me still away. He asked if anyone was still bothering you. He said Richard's not doing so great. I said I understand. It might be the only thing Matt and I have in common.

We're both doing this so you and Richard never have to.

Love,

Joe

June 5, 1944

Dear Charlie,

I have a feeling this will be the last time I can write you for a while. Please don't worry. It means something happened. But it doesn't have to mean something BAD happened.

So . . . I have two confessions, if that's the right word. One about the war, the other about me.

That full-sized rubber tank Matt and I had to transport . . . no, I can't bring it home for you, but I will now tell you what it was for. I don't know if this will get past the censor, but here goes . . .

We're going into France. To get there, we are going to have to cross the English Channel—the body of water between England and France. We wanted to fool Hitler into thinking we were somewhere else in England. That way, the Nazis wouldn't be waiting at the REAL invasion spot. So the Allies came up with a doozy of a plan.

We created a fake army.

And by "fake," I mean "inflatable." The tank Matt and I transported was one of the first, a test. Many more were produced.

It wasn't just tanks. Also boats and planes, and even small buildings, I think. These things were set up to look like a real base, and soldiers were stationed there to act like they would if it were a real base. The idea is that if any German planes flew over, they'd hopefully believe that our forces were bigger and closer than they had thought. Ira said it's like a stage play where the stage is the entire outdoors and the audience is the entire world.

And we think our rubber army worked. We'll find out soon enough.

The other confession is harder . . . even harder than military life, in a way. But I owe this to you.

Maybe I am a good brother, Charlie, but I'm not the man you thought I was. This war is about to get a thousand times more intense and I don't feel any more ready than I did when I got here two years ago. It's not the army's fault. They did the best they could do with me. Don't get me wrong—I'm going to give this my all. But everyone's all is different.

And what gets me hardest of all about this is that I left to protect my country when I could barely protect my family. I tried to help you, but in the end, it didn't quite work, and then I left you on your own. I know coming here wasn't my choice, but that doesn't make it sting less. What I'm trying to say is, whatever happens, Charlie, you have my blessing to stop looking to me as your role model. Instead, pick someone who sets out to do something . . . and then really does it. I want you to grow up to be a guy like THAT.

Wow, I don't feel better now that I told you. But what will never change is that I love you.

Wish me luck.

Joe

AUGUST 2, 1944
CLEVELAND, OHIO
HOME OF SUPERMAN AND
OTHER SUPER THINGS

Dear Joe,

It's all different now. For one thing, this is the last letter I will write you.

People are saying we're going to win this war. But I don't think so. Not because of you and the other soldiers—you did a great job. The reason I don't think we'll win is because so many people have been killed. That doesn't feel like winning to me, even if we do beat the Nazis.

Being out there at war is harder than staying home. But when you're IN the war, people dying is everyday life. I know they don't always die right in front of you, but it's never far. You know how it looked where they died. You know how THEY looked. You get used to it, I bet.

But back home, we don't know. That makes it scarier. It's like monster stories in comic books. When they show the monster, it is not as scary as when they only talk about the monster. Your mind can make things the scariest of all. Like kids who are afraid of what's under the bed. I bet in war, it feels like EVERYTHING is under the bed.

We don't find out who died and when and how until weeks or months after it happened.

When we write a letter to someone, we wonder if that person is already gone. And even folks who haven't lost a son or a husband or a brother are sad, because everyone knows someone who lost someone. Every day, I see people with tears in their eyes. In the market. Just walking down the street. They don't see me see them. I think some of them don't even know they're doing it. For soldiers, dying is everyday life. For us, crying is everyday life.

Even when you were so far away, you always tried to look out for me at home. But then you also always wrote that you're no hero, you're no help. But I know what you are, and you know what? I don't care if you don't agree. There are a lot of mean guys around here. I don't see many big brothers sticking up for little brothers the way you have for me. And you taught me how to do it for myself.

Here's how I know.

I told you about that big storm last winter when we were let out of school early. What I didn't tell you is that when I was walking home by myself, I saw Jed shoveling his driveway even though it was still snowing. I tried to pass without letting him see me see him, but he grabbed the hood of my coat and pulled me backward.

He shoved the shovel at me and said, "Perfect timing. You finish."

I looked to his house and he said his parents weren't home. I said I forgot my mittens in school. He just laughed. Then he asked me if I was going to cry.

I didn't say anything. I just shoveled his stupid driveway while he watched. He looked like he couldn't believe I was really doing it. He even started to feel bad. He didn't say I could stop, but he did offer me his mittens.

I told him that my brother had been shot at and threatened and insulted and hungry and had to sleep in mud and hike at night with a heavy pack for hours and live in fear for months and live without his family for years.

I told him that if you can do all that, I can shovel a driveway with cold hands. I told him I didn't do it because I was scared but because it was the nice thing to do. And I told him not to bother me anymore.

Then I said, "This war is over."

Here's the craziest part. We stood there in silence for a minute, just letting snow fall on us. Somehow, right then, something changed. Jed said something that surprised us both. He said that he respected you for what you did. And then he called you a hero.

I knew that already. And I knew it even before you left home. No matter what you say, I know you're not what you seem to be at first. Like an inflatable tank.

All of us still can't believe it. The war took you from us.

But then it sent you back. I think they called it "honorable discharge."

We are luckier than so many families whose boys did not survive June 6, the invasion of France. Like Matt's family. Poor Richard. I know you and Matt weren't exactly friends, but . . . I'm so sorry.

The doctor thinks you'll be back on your feet in six weeks. You might walk with a limp, but like you said first thing when they brought you home, "I still have my life."

You're probably wondering why I didn't tell you before about what happened with Jed. It's because I told myself that if I wished I could tell you in person, then one day I WOULD be able to tell you in person. But I wrote it down so if you ever forget what I think of you, no matter where I am and where you are, you'll always be able to reread this to remind yourself.

I know you're resting. But nothing is going to stop me from walking down the hall to give this letter to you right now.

Love,
Charlie

During World War II, no ground fighting occurred in the United Kingdom. But that doesn't mean nothing dramatic happened there. Before I researched wartime England, I had never considered the enormity of what we now know as D-Day, the Allied invasion of Nazi-occupied France. The date was June 6, 1944—the day after Joe's last letter. I had never wondered just how the Allies could have trained more than 150,000 troops and sneaked them across the English Channel into Normandy. They had to set out from somewhere! And I knew nothing about the massive—and successful—deception.

Charlie, Joe, Matt, and Cookie weren't real, but inflatable tanks were. The Allied plan to trick Nazi Germany with dummy vehicles was called Operation Fortitude, part of a larger plan called Operation Bodyguard.

Those operation names may sound cool, but this effort is sometimes known by another name that is even cooler: the Ghost Army. With your parents, search "ghost army" and "inflatable tanks WWII" online to see astonishing footage of the real fakes.

What's more, the Allies created *two* fake

armies. The one in this story was in southeast England. The other was in Scotland. And the plans involved more than phony tanks. To increase their chances of fully fooling Hitler, the Allies also used phony radio transmissions and double agents—in this case, people who pretended to spy on the Allies for the Nazis but who were actually spying on the Nazis for the Allies.

The soldiers of World War II were also the historians. Simply by writing letters to their families, they preserved thousands of smaller stories that took place alongside the big events. Most of these young men didn't plan on being authors any more than they planned on being fighters. But their personal letters home captured a side of the war that journalists couldn't. Numerous cities have World War II museums, including New Orleans (home to the National WWII Museum), and some display letters from soldiers. If you get the chance to visit any of these museums, you will almost certainly discover stories as surprising as Joe's.

In real life, soldiers who had a role in Operation Fortitude would not have been able to describe in a letter exactly what they were doing. Therefore, to mention the fake tank in my story, I had to take a liberty. Perhaps that's especially apt here because taking liberty—or rather taking back liberty—is often a driving force of war.

Thank you to Sarah Evans for issuing my

passport (and a time machine) for my trip to 1940s England.

Marc Tyler Nobleman

August 2015

P.S. If you don't know what Eisenhower (the general who pets Cookie) did after the war, you might want to look it up . . .

Marc Tyler Nobleman is the author of *Boys of Steel: The Creators of Superman*, which made the front page of *USA Today*; *Bill the Boy Wonder: The Secret Co-Creator of Batman*, which inspired a TED talk; and *Vanished: True Stories of the Missing*. He has spoken at schools and conferences internationally (from India to Tanzania) and blogs about his adventures in publishing at Noblemania. Follow him on Twitter at @MarcTNobleman.